DEBORAH ELLIS

In From the Cold

Grass Roots Press

First published in 2010 by Grass Roots Press

The Good Reads series is funded in part by the Government of Canada's Office of Literacy and Essential Skills.

Grass Roots Press also gratefully acknowledges the financial support for its publishing programs provided by the following agencies: the Government of Canada through the Canada Book Fund and the Government of Alberta through the Alberta Foundation for the Arts.

Alberta
Foundation
for the Arts

Grass Roots Press would also like to thank ABC Life Literacy Canada for their support. Good Reads® is used under licence from ABC Life Literacy Canada.

Library and Archives Canada Cataloguing in Publication

Ellis, Deborah, date
    In from the cold / Deborah Ellis.

(Good reads series)
ISBN 978–1–926583–25–9

    1. Readers for new literates. I. Title. II. Series: Good reads series (Edmonton, Alta.)

PS8559.L5494I54 2010   428.6'2   C2010–902005–7

Printed and bound in Canada.

Distributed to libraries and educational and community organizations by
Grass Roots Press
www.grassrootsbooks.net

Distributed to retail outlets by
HarperCollins Canada Ltd.
www.harpercollins.ca

To those who love to learn

Chapter One

Mother and daughter hid in the shadows.

"There's no one else here."

Rose kept a grip on her daughter's arm. Hazel was ten years old, and she was more interested in adventure than in safety. "What do we do?"

"Always take one more look," Hazel said.

The two of them peered around the corner and toward the back of the shopping centre parking lot. A streetlight shone down on the giant blue Dumpsters. Hazel was right. No one else was around.

Rose looked up at the high-rise apartment buildings in the area. Someone standing on a balcony or watching from a window could look down and see them. She tugged on the front brim of her daughter's baseball cap, lowered her own, then led the way.

They both wore dark jeans and jackets and carried large cloth bags over their shoulders. In her hand, Rose held an extra bag that could expand, in case the haul was especially good.

By now, they were good at climbing. Rose was up the side of the first Dumpster and had the lid back in a flash, without making any noise.

They spoke in whispers, sorting through one Dumpster together before going on to the next. Hazel often wanted to split up, but Rose was too afraid of what she might find. People threw things in Dumpsters that they hoped would never be seen again.

"I see bread," Hazel said.

"Whole wheat?"

"White, I think."

"Take it for now." They'd throw it away later if they found something healthier. Rose put apples and oranges into her bag, along with a battered box of Fruit Roll-Ups and some kind of cereal.

The next Dumpster gave them a carton with half a dozen eggs — only one was broken — and some cottage cheese that had only just expired.

"Look!" Hazel held up a large Toblerone chocolate bar. It looked to be in perfect shape, except for the torn wrapper. Hazel added it to her bag.

"Shh! Someone's coming!"

The two of them stopped sorting. They could hear voices coming nearer.

"Hide or run?" Hazel whispered.

Rose could not decide. She and Hazel always found a lot of free food in these Dumpsters, but the neighbourhood was full of people with nothing to do. Bored people could be dangerous.

She hesitated too long. The voices were now right outside their Dumpster.

"Take the first one," a young man's voice said. "I'll look in here."

And then a face appeared over the side of the Dumpster, the face of a young man with messy hair. He didn't have a chance to blink before Rose and Hazel let out loud, crazy yells. Hazel threw something at the man's face. He screamed, clutched at his eyes, and fell to the pavement.

Rose grabbed her daughter. In the next moment they were out of the Dumpster, running madly and disappearing back into the shadows.

"What did you throw?" Rose asked as they ran.

"Orange juice," Hazel said.

Once they knew they were not being chased, they relaxed enough to laugh, briefly, before continuing with their treasure hunt.

Chapter Two

"Oh, good. Carmen is working."

Donut Heaven was their last stop for the night. They only went inside when they saw that Carmen was behind the counter.

Hazel opened the door. Carmen greeted Rose and her daughter with a big smile and a friendly "*Hola!*"

The donut shop was nearly empty. A man sat with his head on his arms at a table in the back corner. A college student leaned over her laptop computer. Neither looked up at Rose and Hazel.

"I have a present for you, Carmen," Hazel said. She plopped her full shoulder bag down on the counter and opened the zipper of the small pocket on the side. She took out a bracelet with red stones that she'd found in a bag outside the Salvation Army.

"Oh, that's beautiful," said Carmen. She put it on her wrist. "*Muchas gracias.*"

"*De nada,*" said Hazel. "Teach me a new word."

"Say please," said Rose.

"Please."

Carmen taught Hazel a new Spanish word every time they saw each other. Rose left them to the lesson and went to the small stack of newspapers on top of the garbage bin. She quickly checked through them. After all this time, she didn't expect to see anything, but she felt better after she looked.

"Coffee or hot chocolate?" Carmen asked Rose.

Rose preferred coffee, but she wanted to be able to sleep later. "Chocolate. Thanks." She joined her daughter at the counter. She curled her cold fingers around the warm cup.

Carmen put a bag of day-olds beside Rose.

"Muffins and donuts tonight," Carmen told her.

"You are a life saver."

"It's getting colder out," said Carmen.

"We're fine," Rose said.

Carmen left them to take care of a new customer. They finished drinking their hot chocolate, and then Rose got the key to the women's washroom.

"It's too cold to wash my hair tonight," Hazel said.

Rose almost gave in to her, but she didn't know when their next chance to get clean would be. "We're both washing our hair," she said.

They both had short hair, although Rose would need a cut soon. It had been ages since she had been to the hairdresser's.

Hazel fussed, but she bent her head over the small bathroom sink. Rose ran water over Hazel's hair and added hand soap from the soap dispenser. She worked it into a lather, rinsed, then tried to get most of the water out with paper towels.

She washed her own hair, then the two of them did their best to wash the rest of themselves with soapy paper towels.

"My boss is cutting back my hours," Carmen said, as Rose and Hazel stopped by the counter to say goodbye. "He's talking about putting me on the day shift."

Rose was not happy to hear that. No Carmen meant no more free hot chocolate and donuts. Even worse, it meant no safe place to wash, and no regular way of checking the newspapers.

"I hope that doesn't happen," Rose said.

"Me, too," said Carmen. "I can't pay my bills if I work less hours. I'll have to find another job."

Rose and Hazel said goodbye. They left the comfort of the warm donut shop and headed back out into the chilly, dark night.

Chapter Three

Rose and Hazel were both bone tired by the time the city sky turned from black to purple. The rest of the night had passed without incident, apart from ducking out of sight when a police car drove by. The hunting had been good, and they were burdened with their treasures. All they had to do now was make it safely home.

Always, on these journeys, Rose wished she were two people. She had to walk in front of Hazel, to protect her from anything that was ahead, but she also wanted to walk behind. What if something — someone — snatched at her daughter as they walked by?

Most of the city was asleep at this hour. The pre-dawn air was cold, as if to encourage people to stay home under the covers.

A large river valley cut through the middle of the city. In the richer areas, this ravine was steep and narrow, with a concrete pathway at the bottom for dog-walkers and joggers. There were streetlights in those parts of the valley to keep the joggers safe at night.

In other spots, the ravine opened up to a wide area of waste land, stretches of undeveloped scrub brush. The river widened there, with weeping willow trees hanging over it.

Rose and Hazel crossed a footbridge over some train tracks. They left the sidewalk and headed down a dirt path into the long grass of the waste land. They had half a kilometre to go before they reached their shack. The streetlights didn't reach the waste land. Rose and Hazel had to walk in the dark.

Rose would have felt better if they could sing while they walked, but she knew there were others living in their ravine. It was safer not to disturb them. So they walked almost in silence.

Rose only whispered to her daughter now and then to make sure Hazel was still with her.

By now, Rose knew each group of trees, each clump of brush. She knew when to leave the open area and walk into what looked like thick bushes until she lifted away the branches and uncovered the trail. Their hut had been harder to find before the season changed and the leaves fell from the trees.

She waited for Hazel to get in front of her, then she put the branches back in place, like closing a gate.

Their shack could now be seen. It, too, was covered with branches, but they could not hide the blue plastic tarp, draped over the old boards and windows leaning into each other. It was a sturdy little shack, built from things other people had thrown away.

The walls were wooden skids, stolen from warehouse yards late at night. Rose and Hazel had carried big pieces of particle board from a construction site to add to the wood from the skids. Everything was covered with plastic to keep the rain out.

Rose did not waste time admiring the shack. She looked for signs that it had been disturbed.

The row of empty soda cans lined up in front of the door was knocked over.

"Hold it," she whispered.

This had happened before. The wind, or an animal, had disturbed the cans. It was probably the same this time. But Rose had to check to make sure.

"Mom," complained Hazel, her arms full and aching.

"Shh. Wait."

Rose carefully pried open the board they used as a door and peered inside the hut.

Someone was sleeping on the floor.

Rose dumped her armload of treasures. "Get down!" she yelled at Hazel, then she leapt into the hut, grabbing the thick stick that they kept just inside the door.

"Get out of here! Get out!"

The person on the floor was an old man, hairy and scruffy. He stumbled to his feet, stinking of alcohol and filth from the street.

"I'm just sleeping," he said, in a sound that was part roar and part mumble. His words slurred together.

"Get out! Out!"

Rose waved the stick at him. She wanted badly to hit him. In his drunken state, it would be so easy to knock him to the ground. But then she'd have a knocked-out drunk on her hands. She just wanted him to go, and to scare him enough so that he wouldn't come back.

"Get out!"

He ran out. Rose chased after him, pounding the ground every time he showed signs of slowing down. When he was a good distance away, she stopped chasing him and threw stones at his retreating back.

"Hazel? Where are you?"

Hazel stood up. She had been hiding behind a clump of tall, dead weeds.

"You said no one would find us," Hazel shouted. "You said we would be safe."

"It's just that it's fall," Rose said. "The leaves are gone, and we're not so well hidden anymore."

"So what are we going to do, then?"

Rose was tired. "I chased him away, didn't I? I'll bet you didn't think your old mom had it in her."

It was a feeble joke, but it was the best Rose could do just then. She didn't want Hazel to know how scared she was.

Hazel had her sulk-face on. She looked exactly as she did when she was two years old.

Not another bad mood, thought Rose. She nodded for her daughter to go inside. Hazel picked up her bags and went into the hut.

Chapter Four

———

"Shoes off," Rose said.

Hazel peeled off her shoes without untying them first, something Rose hated her to do. It stretched the shoes, and who knew when they would find another pair? But Rose held her tongue. She had decided to be less of a nag. Hazel didn't pay attention to nagging, anyway, so they might as well have a little peace.

They put their bags down. Layers of tarp covered the dirt floor of the hut, with flattened cardboard boxes spread over the tarps. On top of the cardboard were pieces of carpet taken from a Dumpster.

"It doesn't look like he stole anything," Rose said.

"He just stunk up the place," said her daughter. "The smell will go away."

Hazel had a bed, a single mattress up on some boards and milk crates. The mattress came from the trash pile outside someone's house on garbage pick-up day. Rose wrapped it in plastic garbage bags before she allowed Hazel to sleep on it.

Rose slept on the floor, on a mattress made from extra pieces of carpet. Their blankets came from bags left on the front step of the Salvation Army in the middle of the night.

Hazel flopped down on her bed and pulled the blankets up over her head.

"You're not going to help me unpack?" Rose asked.

Hazel huffed and got up off the bed.

"I'm not happy with your attitude lately," Rose said. "You used to help without complaining so much."

Hazel didn't answer. She bent low over her sack and started pulling things out. Her bed was soon loaded with books, sweaters, socks, and packages of food.

"You want mice in your bed?"

Hazel took the food and put it on the piece of particle board they used as a table. The square of board, peeling at the corners, was propped up on bricks and covered with a piece of red cloth. A jar usually held wild flowers, but Rose noticed they hadn't picked new ones in a while. The jar now held just stems and dead leaves. The flowers had died, and neither mother nor daughter had bothered to replace them.

This is not good, Rose thought. I have to try harder. I can't let us get sloppy. This may be a shack, but it is still our home.

Hazel still wasn't talking. Rose let her be quiet. Silence was the only way they had any privacy. For four months, neither had been out of the other's sight. Rose hated for Hazel to be more than an arm's length away, so she could always grab her.

The food haul was good. Rose built up a tiny fire, just outside the hut, and cooked all five eggs together, scrambling them without oil or butter. She cut up two of the less-battered oranges and then brought all the food back into the shack.

"Wash your hands," she said to Hazel.

Hazel was back on her bed, thumbing through the books she'd found.

"While it's hot," said Rose.

Hazel left the books and squirted hand sanitizer into the palms of her hands. Rose did the same, and they sat on cushions in front of the low table.

They ate directly from the pan. Rose let Hazel eat most of the eggs.

At least she's eating, Rose thought. She's safe and she's eating.

Rose ate the eggs that Hazel didn't want, and she finished the orange pieces that Hazel was too full to eat.

It was usually Hazel's job to clean up, but Rose did not trust her daughter's new moody attitude. She did the cleaning herself. She took the food scraps out into the bush and covered them with dirt. Then she went to the river's edge with the frying pan.

She was careful not to step on the little toy village Hazel had set up among the tree roots and rocks. Little McDonald's toys from the Salvation Army, Disney figurines, tiny Care Bears, and cars were arranged around houses made of twigs and garbage. Hazel had even built a little marina, with tiny hand-made boats she could sail.

Rose squatted down and scrubbed the pan in the river.

The distant sounds of the busy city waking up drifted down to Rose's ears. What was it the nuns used to say? Be *in* the world but not *of* the world. Rose was in the city, the city she'd lived in all her thirty-one years, but she was no longer a part of it. The quiet around her was an unexpected blessing of their new life.

"The water's dirty," Hazel said.

Rose jumped at the sound and got to her feet. Hazel was watching her.

"The heat from the fire kills any germs," Rose told her.

"How do you know?"

"What?"

"You say that like you know. How do you know? Did you do a germ test? In school, in science class, we did experiments to prove something. Did you do that?"

"Yes," Rose lied. "At university."

"You studied history at university."

"There was a required science course. Heat from fire destroys germs from water."

"All the germs?"

"Yes. All the germs."

Rose did not like the look on Hazel's face. It was not defiance, or anger, or even sadness. Rose could not identify the look, but she did not like it.

She shook the water out of the pan and headed back to the shack. "Let's get some sleep," she said.

"I'm not tired."

"Well, I am."

Rose held her breath until she heard Hazel fall into step behind her.

At least she's still obeying, Rose thought.

Their outdoor latrine was a hole in the ground, surrounded by boards to step on. An old shower curtain hung from the trees provided some privacy. They'd used the washroom in the donut shop before heading back to the shack, so they didn't need to use their latrine now.

Hazel's pillow was near a window. She picked up one of her new books and turned her back to her mother.

Rose piled up the carpet pieces and got her blankets out of the garbage bag that kept out the damp. She made up her bed. Before crawling into it, she got the long piece of string from the hook. She looped one end around her ankle then took hold of Hazel's foot.

Hazel kicked her away.

Rose took hold of her foot again.

Hazel kicked again and snorted out a whine.

"Enough!" said Rose.

Hazel finally allowed the string to be tied around her ankle.

There. They were joined together.

No one could steal her daughter without her knowing.

Rose crawled into her blankets. The floor still stank of the intruder, but she could ignore that. She closed her eyes and prayed she wouldn't have a nightmare.

Chapter Five

Rose fought off waking up.

As long as she was asleep, everything was fine. She was dreaming of something good, something safe. If she could just hold onto it…

But it was gone. She was awake.

She opened her eyes and tried to guess how much time had passed. It was a game she played with herself. Three hours? Four hours? She couldn't remember the last time she'd had eight hours of solid sleep.

Four hours, she decided, then looked at her watch. Off by half an hour.

Hazel was still asleep, curled up facing the wall.

Coffee and a cigarette — that's what Rose would have. She didn't like to smoke in front of her daughter. Long cigarette butts tossed onto the sidewalk or stuffed into public ashtrays made up her small stash of smokes. The ashtrays in front of hospitals and office towers were the best places to find these butts. She kept a few in a plastic bag, as a rare treat for when she was awake and Hazel was not.

Rose reached for her sweater and pulled it on as she stepped out of the shack to build up the fire.

They kept their fire in a big pot, covering it with a lid when it wasn't needed. Just a bit of air going in and out kept the coals going. They were still warm from breakfast. Rose added twigs and newspaper and wondered if she would dare bring it inside when winter came.

The flames caught the paper, and in the same instant Rose realized she was walking freely, unattached to her daughter. The string was still around her ankle, but it trailed along the ground beside her.

In two leaps, she was inside the shack, at Hazel's bed, shaking her daughter awake.

The pillows lost their form in Rose's hands. They had been laid out, under the covers, to look like a sleeping child.

Rose clamped her hand over her mouth to keep the screams inside.

She must not panic. Hazel was probably just being disobedient. Her daughter was getting more wilful by the day, and Rose was really going to have to put a stop to it. Hazel was only ten, way too young for teenager attitude.

Rose first checked their outdoor toilet.

"Hazel?" she called out quietly, then she pushed aside the shower curtain. No Hazel.

She's probably down by the river, Rose thought. She can spend hours down there, sailing those hand-made boats of hers, but she can't spend five minutes washing dishes. That was something else that was going to change.

Rose headed down the short path to the river. She blamed herself for being slack about discipline. This new life of theirs wasn't easy, but they were used to it now, and there was no reason why Hazel couldn't start behaving better.

But the clearing by the river was empty. No Hazel.

Rose went back to the shack. Now she *needed* that cigarette!

She built up the fire again. She poured water into a metal mug from the plastic bottle she'd refilled in the donut-shop washroom and added instant coffee. Her supply was getting low. They'd have to do another shoplifting trip soon, for coffee, hand sanitizer, and matches. She put the metal cup right into the fire to make the water boil faster and fed more sticks into the flames.

A punishment, that's what Hazel needed. In their old life, Rose could have taken away television or time with friends, but there was none of that left to take away.

The Toblerone bar! Hazel was so excited to find it last night, and she would be looking forward to eating it. Well, she wouldn't get it! Rose had to let her know that Mom was still in charge.

Rose went to the shelf where she'd put the chocolate bar. The chocolate was not there.

Rose was getting madder by the minute. Madder and more afraid. They had been living this way for four months, and Hazel had never pulled a stunt like this before.

Rose got her bag of cigarette butts out and sat on the log by the fire pot. She smoked three butts, lighting a new one from the end of the one before it. She wasn't used to smoking. The nicotine buzzed in her brain.

The coffee was hot enough to taste almost like coffee. What should I do? Rose wondered as she drank. Should I go look for her? Should I stay here and wait for her to come home?

Rose didn't know where she would even begin to look.

Unless…unless Hazel tried to go back to the house. Their old house.

Rose could not stand that thought. Hazel would *not* go back there! She was probably just off wandering or stretching her legs, or hiding.

Rose jumped into action. She circled the camp, from the river, around the shack, then back to the river. She widened the circle, looking in clumps of tall grass and in clusters of bushes.

"I've been saving up our loose change," she called out. "I was thinking of going to McDonald's tonight. What do you say?"

There was no answer.

Rose was not used to being away from the shack in daylight. It began to bother her. She was out in a field, in a big piece of waste land, but the city was all around. High-rise apartments rose out of the hills on the other side of the river. Rose imagined that the windows were lined with people, looking down at her, watching her.

She gave up the search and fled to her shack. She curled up on Hazel's bed and stared out the window, willing her daughter to come back.

Chapter Six

The sun had shifted the shadows around the shack when Rose finally saw Hazel coming up the path.

Hazel was walking quickly. She saw her mother's frowning face at the window, stopped, then continued more slowly.

Rose met her outside the shack. The hours of waiting had made her more angry and more frightened. Her rage and her fear took over her good sense. She came at her daughter with her hand raised in the air. The hand came down with a fury, smacking Hazel across the face and sending the girl sprawling into the dirt.

"Get up!" shouted Rose, as Hazel lay where she fell. "Get up and face me! Do you know what you put me through?"

Rose grabbed Hazel by the jacket shoulders, lifted her to her feet, then slapped her again into the dirt.

"You do not leave!" Rose yelled. "You know that. Why did you leave? Where did you go?"

"I just…"

"I don't care what you have to say," Rose said. "You don't care about me! I do all of this!" Rose waved her hands at the shack made out of trash. "I do all of this for *you*, to protect *you*, and you repay me by running off the first chance you get."

Rose was so mad now that she could not see straight. The world around her was a blur. Her daughter, on the ground, was a blob, without clear form or lines. Rose wanted to keep hitting her. She wanted to pound her daughter until the horrible feelings were all pounded out of her.

"Get to your feet!"

Rose reached down again and grabbed the girl. Hazel made her body limp and heavy. Rose tried to lift her, then felt a muscle twitch and pull in her back. Pain stretched through her entire body.

She let go of Hazel. Hazel dropped back to the ground with a thud.

"My back!" Rose gasped.

The pain was terrible.

This can't be happening, she thought. Not now. Not here.

She'd had this back problem before, and it was awful. But back then she'd had a warm house and pain pills and a proper bed to help her out. Even then, there had been weeks when simply getting out of bed and walking to the toilet had been terrible because of the pain.

"My back. Help me!"

Her daughter stayed on the ground. Rose saw Hazel watching her. There was almost no emotion in her daughter's face. She did not seem to care that her mother was in agony.

"You are a monster," Rose said. "Help me, or I'll…"

"Or you'll what?" Hazel asked.

That lip again. The girl needed to be brought under control before she became a teenager.

What if she won't help me? Rose thought, and for a brief moment, the fear of that jolted through her body. The fear went to her face.

Hazel saw it. Rose could tell by Hazel's new look of power.

Rose tried to get control back by ordering her daughter to stop fooling around on the ground and get up and help her, but it was too late. The power shift happened in only a moment, but that moment changed everything.

Rose held her breath.

Hazel got up and stood by her mother. Rose leaned on her. Step by careful step, they went into the shack. Hazel eased Rose onto the bed, helped her lie down, and remained standing in front of her.

They stayed like that, in silence, for a good long while.

Then Hazel took a blanket and gently covered her mother. After that, she sat down on the floor.

"Take your shoes off," Rose said, with her eyes closed against the pain.

"Yours are still on." But Hazel took off her shoes, got up and took off her mother's, and then went back to her spot on the floor.

"What was so important that you had to cause me so much worry?" Rose asked.

"It's Emma's birthday."

Rose opened her eyes in alarm. "You didn't go to see her?"

"I just went to the school. She's my best friend. It's her birthday! I took her the Toblerone bar."

"You have ruined everything. Did they see you? They must have seen you."

"They were at an assembly. I left the chocolate bar on her desk," Hazel said.

"With a note?"

"I had to leave a note. Or she wouldn't have known it was from me."

Rose tried to get off the bed, but the smallest movement gave her more pain. "You risked it all for a stupid birthday."

"It's not a stupid birthday! It's my best friend's birthday!"

"Childhood friendships don't matter," Rose said. "Adult friendships don't even matter. Emma has probably forgotten all about you."

Hazel was crying, saying that wasn't true, but Rose knew. No one could be depended upon. The sooner Hazel learned that, the better.

Then she had another thought. "How did you know it was Emma's desk?"

Hazel tried to stop crying. "What?"

"How did you know where Emma sits? You hung around the school, didn't you? You talked to the teachers, didn't you?"

"No! No, I swear."

If Rose could have looked her daughter full in the face, she'd know for sure whether Hazel was lying or not. But her daughter was looking off to the side, and Rose's back would not allow her to twist around to see. "I don't believe you," she said.

"I didn't talk to anybody. Emma is in Mrs. Sampson's class. I saw her through the window, before they went to the assembly."

"You stood and watched through the window? And nobody saw you? You're lying."

"I'm not lying," Hazel said.

"Then how did you get into the school? It's locked during the day. You have to be buzzed in."

"I just — I just made up a name. I said I was late, and they let me in. I said I was Devon. We have four Devons in my class. In what used to be my class."

Rose had to admit that her daughter was clever. Too clever. That kind of cleverness could get them caught.

"You really should grow up," Rose told her. "All that fuss over a child's birthday. Did you write on the note where we're living? Did you draw her a map?"

"It's none of your business what I wrote, but I'll tell you. I wrote, 'Happy birthday to the best friend ever, love, Hazel.'"

I should have remembered her friend's stupid birthday, Rose thought. I could have thought of something safe for Hazel to do.

"It looked like they were doing cool stuff in science," Hazel said. "About the insides of animals and how all the parts work together. And there was an arithmetic problem on the board that I don't know how to do."

"Be quiet now, and let me rest."

"School started only two months ago," Hazel said, "and already I'm falling behind."

"I said, be quiet. Can't you see I'm in pain?"

Hazel kept talking. "I could go to a different school, and use a different name."

"No, you couldn't."

"Why not?"

"Because you have to have files. You have to have papers. You have to have come from somewhere. Now, do I have to ask you again to let me have some quiet?"

Rose had her quiet, almost a full minute of it.

Then Hazel spoke again. Quietly. Almost under her breath. "You don't know everything. You can't even walk right now. I can do what I want to, and you can't stop me."

Rose kept her eyes shut and her mouth closed and did not rise to the bait.

"I'm supposed to be in school," Hazel muttered. "It's the law."

"Shut up," said Rose.

"It's like I'm being punished," said Hazel. "I don't see why *I* should be punished."

She was silent for a moment. Then she said, "After all, I wasn't the one who killed Daddy."

Chapter Seven

Neither Rose nor Hazel had spoken about that awful night since it happened.

Rose had hoped — prayed — that Hazel had been asleep. At first, she'd been puzzled that Hazel hadn't asked about her father. Four months had gone by, and not a mention. Now, that made sense. Hazel knew her father was dead.

"It was an accident," Rose said.

Hazel turned around on the floor until her back was to her mother.

"Honey, it was an accident," Rose said again. "I didn't mean to."

Hazel didn't reply.

Now she decides to keep quiet, Rose thought. "I don't know what you think you saw."

"What I *saw*," said Hazel.

"I'm sorry that you saw anything."

It had been a bad night. No worse than other nights, except at the end.

He had been drinking, of course, and he was angry about something. He was always angry about something, and Rose couldn't remember now what had set him off on that last night. Was it something she'd said? Was it something she'd failed to say? Something wrong with the food at supper?

He had a talent for finding things wrong. And she never did anything as simple as make a mistake. Shoes not lined up meant she was not respecting him. Agreeing with the prime minister when her husband disagreed meant she was being disloyal. Not laughing at something her husband thought was funny meant she was cold. Laughing at a male comedian's joke meant she wanted to sleep with that comic. Laughing at a female comedian's joke meant she was a man-hating bitch. She needed to have the attitude beaten out of her.

There was no way to win. Silence was safest. Silence and agreement. She'd learned to watch his face for clues and to listen hard to his tone of voice. Sometimes she was able to head off his anger. But if he was in a hitting sort of mood, nothing would stop him.

The beating wasn't the worst part. The beating came at the end, the final burst of bad energy at the end of a bad night. He'd hit, he'd kick, he'd throw things, he'd slam her head against the wall. Bad. Bad.

But then it would be over. She'd see it in his face. The tension would leave his eyes. He'd mutter something like, "You shouldn't push me like that," then he'd sit on the sofa and turn on the television.

Or, if he was really drunk, he'd just flop into bed and fall asleep. That was the best, those hours of silence. She could ice down her sore spots, put the house back together, and make sure Hazel was all right.

Worse than the beating was what led up to it. On and on, he'd go on and on with his criticisms, accusing her of some crime or other. If she tried to defend herself, he'd twist her words around, so that everything she said somehow made it worse. If she tried to stay silent, hoping that would make it all go away, he would go after her for her silence.

"You think you're so pure," he'd yell, right into her face. "You think you're such a victim."

Hazel was supposed to stay in her room whenever she heard her father's voice getting loud.

"You go into your room, you close the door, and you keep it closed," Rose told her. "Whatever is happening below is none of your business."

"What if I need to pee?" she asked one time.

Rose gave her large, plastic ice-cream tubs to keep in her closet in case of such emergencies. She also kept a cookie tin full of snacks under her daughter's bed, and bottles of water for Hazel to drink. Sometimes the yelling went on for a long time. She didn't want her little girl to be hungry.

That last night was an ordinary night.

The same ranting. The same screaming. The same spitting. Rose remembered Hazel taking her plate of macaroni and cheese out of the dining room and up the stairs to her bedroom.

Rose had heard of husbands like hers going after their children. Her own husband, thankfully, ignored Hazel. As long as Hazel was silent, to her father she was invisible.

No, that's not fair, Rose corrected herself. There were times when he was a good father, before the drinking got so bad. He'd read to her, play with her, and put her up on his shoulders when they walked down the street. He could be pleasant sometimes. Rose just had to watch for when he'd had enough, and get Hazel quietly — and safely — out of the way.

Hazel had gone upstairs on that last night. Rose was listening hard to her husband, straining for clues that would tell her how to act. But his temper flared up quickly. She wasn't ready for it.

She couldn't remember now what he said. All she remembered was the screaming, her husband's face large and ugly right in front of her, his spit landing on the skin of her cheeks and forehead. She remembered how loud he was. And she remembered feeling very, very tired, as she tried to retreat into that secret part of her brain to wait out the storm.

She remembered taking her plate into the kitchen. She had the ketchup bottle in her hand when he came at her. Did she squeeze the bottle of ketchup, or did it get squeezed when he hit her?

She didn't know. But somehow ketchup ended up squirting out all over her husband's face.

And then she did the worst thing she could do. She did the thing she knew absolutely that she must never do.

She laughed.

There were blows. There were kicks. There were slaps and punches.

And then there was a knife in her hand.

The knife went into her husband.

And her husband fell to the floor.

Chapter Eight

It's only pain, Rose told herself. You can't die from pain.

The trip to the latrine was almost unbearable. She'd had to lean on Hazel all the way. Rose was determined not to scream. She'd given Hazel a bad enough day as it was.

She remembered there were a few Tylenol left. Hazel got them for her, and got her a drink of water to swallow them with. The pills wouldn't take away the pain in her back, but they would make it feel less severe. She got back on the bed, and Hazel covered her up again.

"Get yourself something to eat, honey," Rose told her.

"I'm not hungry," Hazel said. A moment later, Rose heard her daughter open a box of crackers and twist the lid off the peanut butter jar. Crackers and peanut butter had been Hazel's favourite snack ever since she was a toddler.

"You're not being punished, Hazel," Rose said. "You didn't do anything wrong. Well, you did something very wrong today, but you know what I mean. Living here isn't a punishment."

"It feels like a punishment."

"You used to think it was an adventure."

"It was. It used to be."

"It still is," Rose said. "Don't you like going into the city at night, when everyone else is asleep? Don't you enjoy going treasure hunting with me?"

"I want to get food from a grocery store," Hazel said. "I want to watch television in the evening and sleep in my own room at night. I want to use my library card again. And I want to go back to school."

"One day, honey," Rose said.

"When?"

"Soon."

"But when?"

"Don't pester me."

49

"We could go back to our house today," Hazel said. "Daddy won't be there. Someone would have cleaned him up."

"Hazel!"

"I saw it in the newspapers. Someone found his body and took it away."

"You're not supposed to read newspapers! All that bad news gives you nightmares."

"You can't forbid me to read newspapers," Hazel said. "I'm a citizen. My teacher said it's everybody's job to keep up on current events."

Rose wanted silence. She wanted to keep her eyes closed, huddle under the blanket, and wait for the Tylenol to work. She wanted to have only herself to worry about. She wanted another life.

"It's not that simple," she said. "We can't go back."

"But why can't we?"

"Do you want me to be arrested?" Rose asked. "Because that's what would happen. And you would end up in foster care. Do you want to live with strangers?"

"You said it was an accident."

"It was. But people won't believe me."

Hazel didn't say anything, and Rose started to drift off. The Tylenol was taking the sharp edge off the pain in her back. Maybe this time it wouldn't last too long. After all, she could rest, here in this shack. She didn't have to get up and look after her husband. She could rest and heal and be all right again.

She was almost asleep when Hazel spoke again.

"We could tell people that I did it."

Rose opened her eyes. "What?"

"We could say I killed Daddy. They won't put me in prison. I'm too young."

"Don't talk like that."

Hazel shuffled over to the bed on her knees and leaned in close to her mother. Rose could smell the peanut butter on her daughter's breath.

"I'll say it was an accident," Hazel said. "They'll believe me. I'll say I wanted to get him to stop hitting you, and I grabbed the knife to protect myself, and it went into Daddy by mistake."

"Stop," Rose said, even while she was thinking. She'd thrown the knife into the river. Was there anything, really, that could prove she killed her husband?

Hazel leaned in even closer. Her face was excited, like it used to be when she retold the plot of a movie she really liked.

"I was in the kitchen," Hazel said. "I was putting my plate in the sink. You and Daddy came in. He was yelling and hitting you. I picked up the knife to get him to stop, and I accidentally killed him. Then I got scared and ran out of the house. You came after me to protect me."

Rose was impressed by the detail in her daughter's story.

"How long have you been thinking about this?" she asked.

"I just thought of it now," Hazel said, taking another bite of cracker. "But maybe it's been in my head for a while, waiting to come out. My teacher last year said our brains work like that sometimes. We'll try and try to do something in math, and we can't do it, and then one day it all makes sense."

"You have a good brain," Rose told her, "but your plan won't work. I'll still be in trouble for keeping you out of school, and for other things, too, I'm sure."

"But you won't be in prison," Hazel said. "Please, Mom, can't we go back?"

It's so wrong, Rose thought, but she began, in spite of herself, to feel something like hope. Maybe there was a way out of this.

But no. It was wrong. "I can't let you take the blame," Rose said. "It would be a lie, and I can't let you do it."

Hazel slumped back to the floor. She sat again with her back to her mother.

"I'm going to grow old in this shack, aren't I?" Hazel said. "I'm going to be thirty years old and still living here."

Rose had no comforting words. She had no plans, no ideas, and no thought for anything except to get through another day.

Hazel kept quiet then, and Rose finally fell asleep.

She woke up in the middle of the night, freezing in spite of the blanket. She had to pee, but Hazel was asleep and Rose couldn't make it to the latrine without her.

She was stuck with a full bladder, in the dark and the cold, with nothing to distract her from the slow passing of the minutes.

It was a long, long night.

Chapter Nine

Rose finally drifted off to sleep at some point. And when the sounds of morning entered her brain — the dawn birds, the first wave of traffic into the city — she shut her eyes tighter. She wanted to avoid waking up. Yesterday had been awful. Today would probably not be any better.

After that last fight had ended, and her husband's body lay in a lake of blood and ketchup on the kitchen floor, Rose stopped. She stopped thinking. She stopped feeling. She stopped being able to stand. Her legs gave way and she slid to the floor, away from the blood, and just sat.

She had no clue how long she sat like that. Even now, months later, she didn't know. And she didn't know what had prompted her to get up.

It must have been a noise, she thought. It must have been a noise made by Hazel. Her daughter must have come down to see what all the silence was about.

Always, before, at the end of a fight, Rose would go up and check on Hazel. They'd empty the pee-pot, if necessary. She'd give Hazel a quiet bath, then they'd go back into Hazel's bedroom to play or read as if nothing had happened.

On the last night, Rose hadn't gone upstairs.

Hazel must have been very scared, Rose realized. Maybe she thought we had gone away and left her all alone. Maybe she thought we were both dead.

I must ask her about it, Rose thought. She should get Hazel into counselling. Children could be damaged forever from seeing such things.

But how could she get Hazel to a counsellor? It would be too dangerous. There would be questions — but didn't a doctor have to keep secrets? Maybe there was a way.

Rose gently tried to stretch out her legs to see if her back was still in trouble. It hurt, but she didn't think it was as bad as it was yesterday.

If she could get to a doctor, she could get treatment for her back and help for Hazel. She could use fake names. The doctor could not go to the police. Wasn't that the way it worked?

Rose kept her eyes closed. As long as she didn't open them, she did not have to face the day.

She didn't hear her daughter moving. Hazel was probably still asleep.

If she's gone, thought Rose, I'll leave. I'll walk out of here as best I can. I'll find a tree branch to use as a walking stick. I'll hitch a ride in a car or a truck and go where no one knows me. Hazel will be fine. She'll be taken care of.

Foster homes are better now, Rose thought. Sure, there are some bad apples, but most people are kind, and Hazel is a good kid. If she were treated well, she wouldn't be a problem for anyone. She'd go back to school, get some counselling, and she'd be fine.

And she would no longer be Rose's responsibility. Rose could start again. She'd completed one year of university before dropping out to have Hazel. She'd gotten good grades, too. She was smart. Maybe she'd go out west. She'd head out to Saskatchewan and cross into the United States. The border on the prairies was open, wasn't it? She was only thirty-one. She could start again.

Her mind went back to the night of the last fight.

After Rose got up off the kitchen floor, she pulled the knife out of her dead husband. She wrapped it in a dish towel and put it in her purse. Then she went upstairs.

Did she even speak to Hazel? She didn't remember. She remembered dumping out Hazel's school backpack, getting rid of the notebooks and schoolgirl junk. She refilled it with socks and underwear and a change of clothes. Then she got last year's backpack out of Hazel's closet. It had Tweety Bird's picture on it. Hazel was too old to carry the Tweety Bird pack, so she kept her collection of Archie comics in it. Rose dumped the comics out, took it into her bedroom, and filled it with her own clothes. She remembered toothpaste and toothbrushes, Tylenol, and soap.

She found a bit of money in her husband's top drawer and more cash in his wallet. She left the credit cards. They were in his name, anyway. He would not let her have her own credit card, or her own bank account. She didn't even have her own birth certificate or driver's licence.

"You'll only lose it," he said. He kept all of her identification papers and documents in a safe in the wall that only he could get into. She had a library card and a grocery-store points card. She had no other proof of who she was.

She didn't remember Hazel complaining or asking any questions as they put their shoes and jackets on. Hazel quietly did as she was told. They put on the backpacks and walked out of their house for good. The street was deserted and silent. Unless one of the neighbours was watching from a darkened window, no one saw them leave.

Why hadn't she left the city? She'd grown up here, and except for a school field trip once to Niagara Falls, she'd never left.

I'm only thirty-one, she thought again. There's plenty of time left to see the whole world if I want to.

And she *did* want to! She wanted to see everything and do everything! All she had to do was open her eyes, see that her daughter was gone, and take off by herself.

She was beginning to feel excited.

"Mom?"

That one word dashed all hope.

"Mom? Look outside."

Rose opened her eyes and looked out the window.

The world was white.

A heavy frost had covered the city during the night. It lay on the trees and the grass, making them glisten in the early morning sun. The frost had also crept into their shack. It was on their blankets.

It looked pretty, but it wasn't.

It was the first sign of winter.

Chapter Ten

Everything was cold and covered in frost — their cushions, their furniture, even the insides of their shoes. As it melted, it left everything wet.

The cold was a pain, and it added to the pain in Rose's back. She still needed her daughter's help to get to the latrine.

Hazel was in a bad mood again, and she argued about everything she was asked to do. She walked around their shack and yard with a blanket wrapped around her shoulders, trying to get warm.

"It's dragging in the dirt," Rose said. "Pick up the ends."

"I'm too cold," Hazel replied.

"Then you'll sleep with a dirty blanket tonight."

"No, you will. I want my bed back tonight."

"I can't get down onto the floor with my back like this. You know that. Go find some twigs to get a fire going."

"*You* do it. You're the mother."

"When I tell you to do something, do it, and don't argue."

They carried on like that through the morning. The two of them bumped up against each other and nothing got done.

The pain in Rose's back was bad, but at least she could move a bit more easily. She took the last of the Tylenol. She tried to get a fire going, but the wood was too wet and the flames wouldn't catch. Rose gave that up and mixed herself a cold coffee — instant coffee stirred into cold water. It tasted horrible, but it delivered the caffeine. She took her coffee and sat in the sun, trying to get warm. She smoked one of her cigarette butts and ignored Hazel's whining.

Finally, the sun got some warmth into it, and Rose's mood began to improve.

Her thoughts in bed had taken her to a place of freedom, and she hated to give that up.

"How would you like to go to Vancouver?" she asked Hazel.

Hazel looked up from the book she was reading. "What do you mean?"

"You didn't think we were going to stay here all winter, did you?"

"Vancouver? What's in Vancouver?"

"The winters are warmer there," Rose said. "It hardly ever snows. Besides, it's beautiful."

"Have you been there? Have you seen it?"

"I've seen pictures."

Hazel turned back to her book. "I've seen pictures of this city that make it look beautiful, too."

"Well, get used to the idea, because that's what we're doing."

"Will we have to live in a shack?" Hazel asked.

"Maybe just at first," Rose said, "but only for a little while. I'll get a job, and you'll go to school."

"I can go back to school?" asked Hazel. "But what about my files? You said I needed papers to go to school."

"We'll say you were in school in Nova Scotia, and the files haven't caught up to you yet. If you behave yourself, they won't ask questions."

"I'll behave. When can we go? How are we going to get there?"

"We'll go just as soon as my back feels a little better. We might even go tomorrow. And we'll hitchhike. We'll meet wonderful people all across the country."

Rose could see it in her mind as she talked. They would ride in the warm cabs of trucks with drivers who told stories. They'd ride in cars, in the back seats of retired couples who were finally seeing the country, stopping at Tim Hortons for soup and donuts. They'd even get invitations to spend the night. "We have a spare room you're welcome to stay in," people would say. "A growing girl needs a proper night's sleep."

They would see the trees and rocks of the Canadian Shield, the wide open skies of the prairies, the amazing Rocky Mountains, and, finally, they would see the Pacific Ocean.

"It's not safe to hitchhike," Hazel said. "The police came to our school. They told us a lot of stuff that I don't remember, but I do remember they said not to hitchhike."

"They meant it's not safe for children to hitchhike alone. You'll be safe if you're with me."

The joy that had filled Hazel's face at the thought of going back to school slipped away. "You don't really know what to do," she said.

"I just told you."

"If you can get a job in Vancouver, why can't you get a job here? Why can't I go to school here?"

"Because they know us here," Rose snapped. When Hazel was younger, her questions were easier. "I'm tired of your complaining. I'm tired of trying to do nice things for you. You don't want to go to Vancouver? Fine. No one is forcing you."

Rose tossed the last of the cold coffee out of her cup and went back inside. The sun had not warmed up the inside of the shack. It was still freezing. She got back into Hazel's bed and covered herself up with blankets. Her back felt better when she was lying down.

Please walk away, she silently begged her daughter. Please take the burden of having to take care of you away from me. Please find someone stronger to bring you up.

But Hazel didn't walk away. She came into the hut and lay down on the bed beside her mother.

They passed the day that way. Sometimes they got up to use the latrine or get something to eat, but then they got back into the bed.

They talked a bit. They dozed a bit. But mostly they just spent the day together, touching hands and listening to heartbeats.

By the end of that day, Rose knew what she had to do.

Chapter Eleven

———

The next morning, Rose and Hazel left the shack for the last time.

They'd woken up before sunrise, when the world was all silver and shadow. Rose's back was still sore, but it was much, much better, and together they tidied and swept the yard and the shack. Hazel even put some pretty, dry grass in the vase on the table.

"Do you think someone else will move in?"

"Someone will," said Rose. "Someone who needs a quiet place to hide for a while."

"I wish I had a camera," said Hazel. "I'd like to take a picture to remember it by."

"Let's take a picture with our minds," Rose suggested. They raised pretend cameras to their eyes and fixed the memory of the hut forever in their brains. Then they walked away.

"I don't want you to lie," Rose said to Hazel as they crossed the field on their way into the city. "That story you made up about you being the one to hurt your father. I don't want you to tell them that. Tell them the truth."

"Okay," said Hazel.

"Promise me," said Rose.

"I promise. Can I show them where we lived?"

"You show them with pride, honey. We did something very special, so you hold your head up high when you're talking about it."

They walked some more.

"If you don't like the people they put you with, you speak up," Rose told her as they got closer to the streets and shops. "You are a great kid and you deserve to have great foster parents."

"It won't be forever," Hazel said. "Right? It will be just for a little while."

"That's right," said Rose. "Just a little while."

Rose was scared to go into the city in broad daylight, but she had to do it. It would be safer for her to leave in the middle of the night, but not safer for Hazel. She had to think of her daughter, but her heart pounded as they walked out of the ravine. They joined the morning crowd on the sidewalk.

Their first stop was the donut shop. Carmen was off duty but Rose wrote down the address.

"Check in here from time to time," Rose said. "We'll use this as our mail drop. I'll let you know where I am, and then you can write and let me know where you are."

"Maybe when you get to Vancouver you can finally learn to use a computer," said Hazel. "Then we can send e-mails."

Rose's husband wouldn't let her touch the computer. He said she only wanted to use it so that she could hook up with other men. But her husband was gone now. She could do whatever she wanted to do. The thought made her laugh out loud. The whole world waited for her!

They started walking again. There were people everywhere, and there was so much noise! Cars, buses, people, dogs! Signs and boxes to walk around. Trucks and strollers to watch out for.

"I like it better at night," Hazel said.

"Me, too," said Rose. Then she had a thought. "You're going to have to do what your foster parents tell you to do," she said. "I mean, if it's safe and reasonable. They're not going to be happy if you wander around at night. You'll have to do chores and be polite. If you give them a hard time, they'll start to pass you from home to home, and your life will be very hard."

"I can get along," Hazel said. "Will they make me do a lot of chores?"

"Probably not a lot," Rose told her, "but when they ask, just do them. Don't argue."

"After all, it's just for a little while."

Rose held tighter to her daughter's hand. "Just for a little while."

They kept walking, and then they were back in their old neighbourhood.

Rose felt — she didn't know what she felt, as she walked past familiar shops and houses. She passed the corner store where her husband had bought his newspapers and lottery tickets. She passed the vegetable stand with the oranges, apples, and onions stacked neatly on trays. They walked past the Portuguese bakery with the plates of small custard tarts in the window. Hazel had loved those tarts when she was younger.

They crossed the street that had been their street. A few houses up was the house that had been *their* house. Rose did not turn her head to try to see it. Would it still have police crime scene tape around it? Would it have a For Sale sign in the yard? Would other people be living there now, using her kitchen, enjoying the flowers she had planted in the narrow beds at the front of the house?

That's my old life, she thought. From now on, she would only look ahead.

Two more blocks, and there was Hazel's school. Rose wiped away the tears that had come into her eyes.

This was where she had taken Hazel on the first day of kindergarten. She had stood and watched outside the school that whole first morning in case Hazel needed her.

This was where she had come for parent-teacher interviews and where she had learned that Hazel was one of the smartest kids in the class. This was where she had come to watch Christmas concerts and the third-grade play.

On days when it rained unexpectedly, Rose had waited outside the school with an umbrella.

The two of them had walked home together, sheltered from the weather.

Why didn't I leave then? Rose asked herself. Why didn't I take Hazel, climb onto a bus, and head out of town back then, back before all this happened? We would have left with nothing, but what do we have now? At least we'd be together.

At the edge of the schoolyard, they stopped. Rose checked her watch. "They'll be coming outside for recess soon. Tell me what you're going to do."

"I'm going to find Emma, and together we'll go talk to the principal."

Her friend Emma would help Hazel to feel brave.

"And if Emma isn't at school today?"

"Then I'll go right into the principal's office and start talking. I won't be scared at all."

"Good girl. And what will you say?"

Hazel looked unsure.

"You'll say the truth, honey," Rose reminded her. "Only the truth."

"Where will you be?"

"I'll be watching, to make sure that you're safe and they're treating you well. You won't be able to see me, but I'll be watching."

She wouldn't be. As soon as Hazel hit the playground, Rose was planning to leave. To stand and watch would be too painful. She'd lose her nerve. She'd run and grab Hazel back, and that was something that could not happen.

"I've changed my mind, Mommy," Hazel said suddenly. She started to cry. "I want to stay with you." She threw her arms around her mother. "Let me go to Vancouver with you. I don't mind hitchhiking. Or let's go back to the shack. I'll be good. I'll help out."

A bell rang in the school. Any second now, kids would start zipping around the playground.

"It's just for a little while," Rose said, breathing in the scent of her daughter's hair. She tried to imprint the feel of her daughter's body against her own so she would never forget it.

She heard the sounds of children and saw the schoolyard filling up. She reached behind and unclasped her daughter's hands from the back of her neck.

"Listen to me," she said, drying Hazel's tears. "You are the best daughter in the world, in the whole history of the world. When you get older, you make sure people treat you with respect, all right? And if any man hits you, ever, even just one time, and even if he says he's sorry, you walk away from him."

"Don't tell me that," Hazel said. "That sounds like advice for when I grow up."

"You're right," Rose said. "Tuck it away until you need it. For now, brush your teeth every night before you go to sleep, work hard in school, and remember that I love you."

They were starting to attract attention. Kids were staring and pointing at them in that unembarrassed way kids do.

"Go now," Rose said. "Go find Emma. I'll be watching, but don't look back. Go!"

She turned her daughter around and gave her a little push in the direction of the school.

Hazel just stood there.

"Go!" Rose ordered.

Then Hazel ran. She didn't look back. She kept on running, right to her friend, Emma. Emma squealed, then Hazel squealed, and then they squealed together and hugged.

Rose had to turn away. She walked quickly down the block, turned the corner, and was soon on one of the city's main streets.

She stood on the edge of the sidewalk and watched the traffic go by. When she spotted a police car, she lifted her arms, waved them in the air, and stepped into the street.

The car stopped. She went over to the driver's side. The officer rolled down the window.

"I killed my husband," Rose said. "Four months ago. You're looking for me."

The officer helped Rose into the back of the car. There was a lot of talk on the police radio and between the two officers in the car that Rose didn't listen to. She closed her eyes and thought about her daughter, so happy to see her friend.

The police wrapped up their radio conversation and steered the car back into the moving traffic. They picked up speed and took Rose away.

Good ∎ Reads

Discover Canada's Bestselling Authors with Good Reads Books

Good Reads authors have a special talent—
the ability to tell a great story, using clear language.

Good Reads books are ideal for people

∗ on the go, who want a short read;
∗ who want to experience the joy of reading;
∗ who want to get into the reading habit.

To find out more, please visit
www.GoodReadsBooks.com

∽

The Good Reads project is sponsored by
ABC Life Literacy Canada.

The project is funded in part by the Government of Canada's
Office of Literacy and Essential Skills.

Libraries and literacy and education markets
order from Grass Roots Press.

Bookstores and other retail outlets order from HarperCollins Canada.

Good Reads Series

If you enjoyed this Good Reads book,
you can find more at your local library or bookstore.

2010

The Stalker by Gail Anderson-Dargatz
In From the Cold by Deborah Ellis
Shipwreck by Maureen Jennings
The Picture of Nobody by Rabindranath Maharaj
The Hangman by Louise Penny
Easy Money by Gail Vaz-Oxlade

2011 Authors

Joseph Boyden
Marina Endicott
Joy Fielding
Robert Hough
Anthony Hyde
Frances Itani

*

For more information on Good Reads,
visit **www.GoodReadsBooks.com**

Easy Money
by Gail Vaz-Oxlade

Wish you could find a money book that doesn't make your eyes glaze over or your brain hurt? Easy Money is for you.

Gail knows you work hard for your money, so in her usual honest and practical style she will show you how to make your money work for you. Budgeting, saving, and getting your debt paid off have never been so easy to understand or to do. Follow Gail's plan and take control of your money.

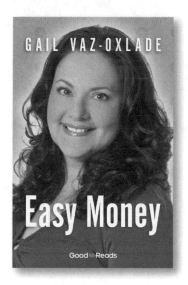

The Picture of Nobody
by Rabindranath Maharaj

Tommy lives with his family in Ajax, a small town close to Toronto. His parents are Ismaili Muslims who immigrated to Canada before Tommy was born. Tommy, a shy, chubby seventeen-year-old, feels like an outsider.

The arrest of a terrorist group in Toronto turns Tommy's world upside down. No one noticed him before. Now, he experiences the sting of racism at the local coffee shop where he works part-time. A group of young men who hang out at the coffee shop begin to bully him. In spite, Tommy commits an act of revenge against the group's ringleader.

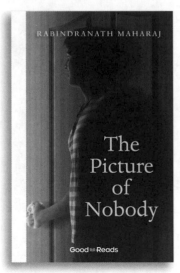

Shipwreck

by Maureen Jennings

A retired police detective tells a story from his family's history. This is his story…

On a cold winter morning in 1873, a crowd gathers on the shore of a Nova Scotia fishing village. A stormy sea has thrown a ship onto the rocks. The villagers work bravely to save the ship's crew. But many die.

When young Will Murdoch and the local priest examine the bodies, they discover gold and diamonds. They suspect that the shipwreck was not responsible for all of the deaths. With the priest's help, Will—who grows up to be a famous detective—solves his first mystery.

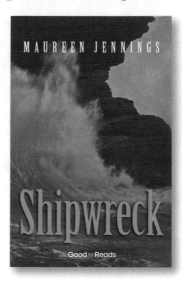

The Hangman
by Louise Penny

On a cold November morning, a jogger runs through the woods in the peaceful Quebec village of Three Pines. On his run, he finds a dead man hanging from a tree.

The dead man was a guest at the local Inn and Spa. He might have been looking for peace and quiet, but something else found him. Something horrible.

Did the man take his own life? Or was he murdered? Chief Inspector Armand Gamache

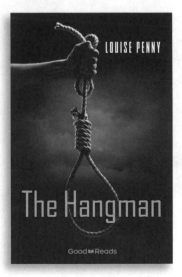

is called to the crime scene. As Gamache follows the trail of clues, he opens a door into the past. And he learns the true reason why the man came to Three Pines.

About the Author

Deborah Ellis is an award-winning author and a long-time peace activist. She has worked as a women's mental health counsellor and volunteered at refugee camps in Afghanistan. Deborah's bestselling series *The Breadwinner Trilogy* is based on a story told to her by a refugee. Deborah lives in Simcoe, Ontario.

Also by Deborah Ellis:

The Breadwinner
Parvana's Journey
Mud City
Women of the Afghan War
The Heaven Shop
I Am a Taxi
Sacred Leaf
No Safe Place

*

The Stalker
by Gail Anderson-Dargatz

Very early one Saturday morning, Mike's phone rings. "Nice day for a little kayak trip, eh?" says the deep, echoing voice. "But I wouldn't go out if I were you."

Mike's business is guiding visitors on kayak tours around the islands off the west coast. This weekend, he'll be taking Liz, his new cook, and two strangers on a kayak tour. Soon, his phone rings again. "I'm watching you," the caller says. "Stay home."

Mike and the others set off on their trip, but the stalker secretly follows them. Who is he? What will he do? *The Stalker* will keep you guessing until the end.

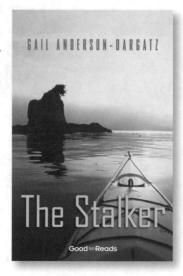